COPYRIGHT

COPYRIGHT ©2020 BY AARON BOWES. ALL RIGHTS RESERVED. NO PART OF THIS BOOK MAY BE REPRODUCED IN ANY FORM BY ELECTRONIC OR MECHANICAL MEANS, INCLUDING INFORMATION STORAGE AND RETRIEVAL SYSTEMS, WITHOUT PERMISSION IN WRITING FROM THE PUBLISHER, EXCEPT BY A REVIEWER WHO MAY QUOTE BRIEF PASSAGES IN A REVIEW.

DEDICATION

TO MY DAUGHTER MELODY FOR BEING MY INSPIRATION

THIS BOOK BELONGS TO

....

Sit back relax let me tell you a story,

This is about a little rapper called Rory,

Rory loves to travel and see new things,

Ceeray is his friend who plays the drum and sings.

Cee-ray, give us a beat to play,

Cee-ray, what shall we do today?

Cee-ray, why don't we go and explore?

So Ceeray and Rory head off on a tour.

The African drum, always starts all the fun,

In the light of the sun, time for exploration,

The rhythm and rhyme, makes everything fine,

By the light of sunshine, its travel time!

Rainforest, the foliage is leafy and green,

Rainforest, greenest place Rory has seen,

Rainforest, biodiversity is high,

And all the natural beauty towers high to the sky.

Rainforest, be amazed by monkeys in the trees,

Rainforest, Ceeray sings to spiders and bees,

Rainforest, hot and humid whilst the rain will pour,

Ceeray plays her drum so they continue the tour.

The African drum, always starts all the fun,

In the light of the sun, time for exploration,

The rhythm and rhyme, makes everything fine,

By the light of sunshine, its travel time!

Dry desert, where the pressure seems to be high,

Dry desert, you hardly get a cloud up in the sky,

Dry desert, where only the toughest survive,

Resilient organisms like cactus will thrive.

Dry desert, can be sandy like the Sahara,

Dry desert, or even icy like Antarctica,

Dry desert, huge camels with adaptations,

Time to leave now so Ceeray plays on her drum.

The African drum, always starts all the fun,

In the light of the sun, time for exploration,

The rhythm and rhyme, makes everything fine,

By the light of sunshine, its travel time!

Cold mountain, frost can bite you under your skin,

Cold mountain, hard to breathe when the air is thin,

Cold mountain, views from these are truly great,

Product of the earth's colliding tectonic plates.

Cold mountain, can be thousands of metres tall,

Cold mountain, Rory shouts and it will echo his call,

Cold mountain, Snowy leopard is hunting its prey,

Ceeray plays her drum to whisk them away.

The African drum, always starts all the fun,

In the light of the sun, time for exploration,

The rhythm and rhyme, makes everything fine,

By the light of sunshine, its travel time!

Vast ocean, supports so many different life forms,

Vast ocean, treacherous when there are big storms,

Vast ocean, our pollution makes it dangerous,

For plants, reptiles, fish, birds and mammals like us.

Vast ocean, are suffering with climate change,

Vast ocean, carbon emissions carry much of the blame,

Vast ocean, full of so much wonder and depth,

Let's look after this world as it's all we have left.

For Rory and Ceeray it's time to say bye,

They're back at home staring at stars in the sky,

Now it's time for their beds so they can get their rest,

And dream about what adventures they can have next.

THE END

Printed in Great Britain
by Amazon

43216434R00015